THE TINY PERFECT
DINOSAUR
BOOK SEVEN

Presenting Hypacrosaurus

by Jennifer Glossop with Dale Russell
Illustrated by Ely Kish

A Somerville House Book

**Andrews McMeel
Publishing**

Kansas City

Contents

This Is Hypacrosaurus 3
The Age of Dinosaurs 4
Family Tree 6
Hypacrosaurus Discovered 8
Other Clues 10
Hypacrosaurus's World 12
Dinosaur Ducks? 14
Why a Crest? 16
Honk, Honk 18
Survival of the Fittest 20
All the Better to Eat With 22
Getting Around 24
Bringing Up Baby 26
Safety in Numbers 28
A Sudden End 30
Farewell to Hypacrosaurus 32

Hypacrosaurus's long head ended in a mouth shaped like a duck's bill. On top of its head was a hollow crest, and down its back ran a sail-like ridge. This tall ridge gave *Hypacrosaurus* its name, which means "very high lizard."

This Is Hypacrosaurus

Hypacrosaurus (hi-PAK-row-sore-us) was a large plant-eating dinosaur that was about twelve feet (3.5 m) tall at its hips—taller than two grown men, one standing on the other's shoulders. Other dinosaurs were bigger and smarter and stronger and fiercer, but more fossil bones and skeletons of *Hypacrosaurus* and its relatives—the duck-billed dinosaurs—have been found than of any other dinosaurs. Without horns or claws or spikes, how did *Hypacrosaurus* manage to survive so well for millions of years?

The Age of Dinosaurs

Dinosaurs lived on the earth from 225 to 65 million years ago, a period called the Mesozoic (mez-oh-ZO-ik). At the beginning of the Mesozoic, the only land on the earth was one huge island called Pangea (pan-GEE-ah). The weather was much warmer than it is now and tended to remain the same all year around. Early dinosaurs were meat-eaters like *Eoraptor* (ee-o-RAP-tor) and plant-eaters like *Pisanosaurus* (pie-SAN-o-sore-us). Later, Pangea began to divide into parts. The weather remained warm, and plants like ferns and cycads thrived. With these

TRIASSIC | **JURASSIC**

Pisanosaurus

plants came larger and mightier dinosaurs like *Brachiosaurus* (BRACK-ee-oh-sore-us) and *Stegosaurus* (STEG-oh-sore-us).

By the end of the Mesozoic, dinosaurs ruled the land. Duck-billed dinosaurs, or hadrosaurs, the family of dinosaurs that *Hypacrosaurus* belongs to, were so numerous that thousands of them often lived together. They had spread all over the earth and were especially common in North America and Asia.

CRETACEOUS

Stegosaurus

Hypacrosaurus

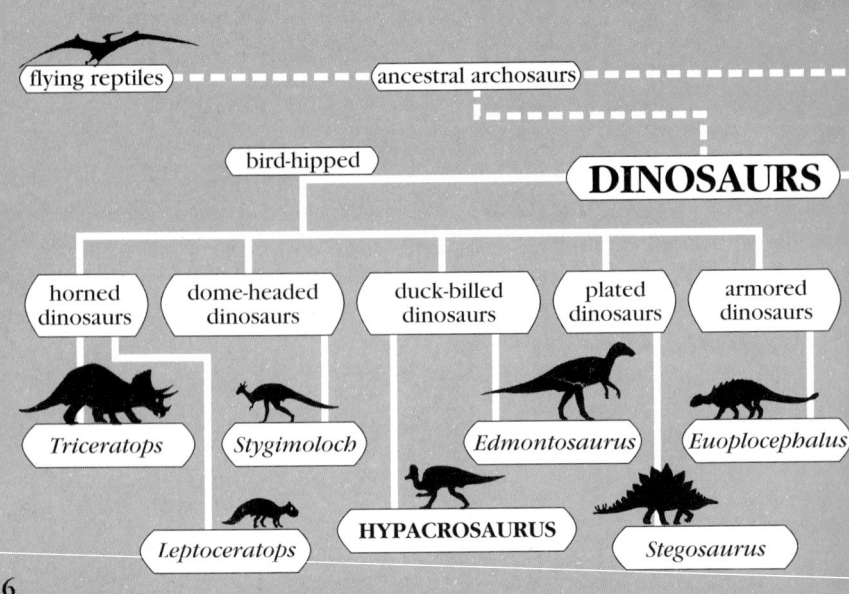

Family Tree

Paleontologists (PAY-lee-on-TAW-lo-jists), scientists who study fossils, classify dinosaurs into groups. Here are some of the famous dinosaurs and the groups they belong in. *Hypacrosaurus* belonged to a group called hadrosaurs, or duck-billed dinosaurs.

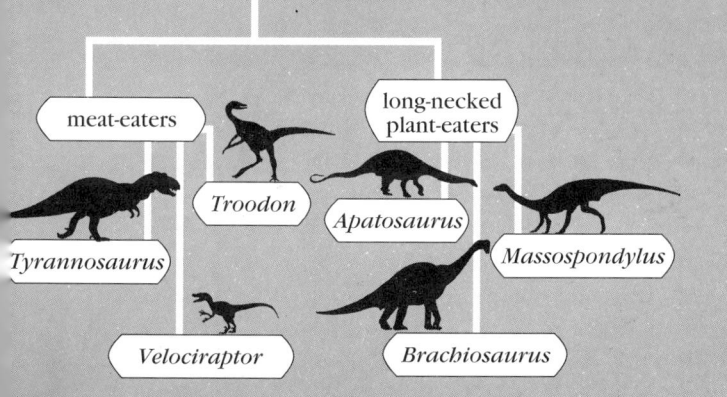

- crocodiles and alligators
- lizard-hipped
  - meat-eaters
    - *Tyrannosaurus*
    - *Troodon*
    - *Velociraptor*
  - long-necked plant-eaters
    - *Apatosaurus*
    - *Brachiosaurus*
    - *Massospondylus*

Hypacrosaurus Discovered

A wounded *Hypacrosaurus* lies down by a stream and dies. The body is soon covered by sand and the flesh rots, until only the bones remain. As the years pass, more and more sand piles on top. Minerals seep into the bones and they harden. Finally, the sand and the bones turn to rock.

The first *Hypacrosaurus* fossils were discovered in 1913 by an American fossil hunter named Barnum Brown. The Red Deer River in Alberta, Canada, was a splendid location for finding fossils since the river had worn away rock, exposing the remains of many dinosaurs. At the time, however, it was not an easy area to reach. Brown solved the problem by floating down the river on a barge. He also discovered lots of other dinosaurs including *Leptoceratops* (LEP-toe-SERR-a-tops) and *Corythosaurus* (ko-RITH-oh-sore-us), a close relative of *Hypacrosaurus*.

Other Clues

Fossils of bones are not the only clues that tell us about dinosaurs and how they lived. Scientists have found fossils of footprints, of eggs, and of baby dinosaur bones.

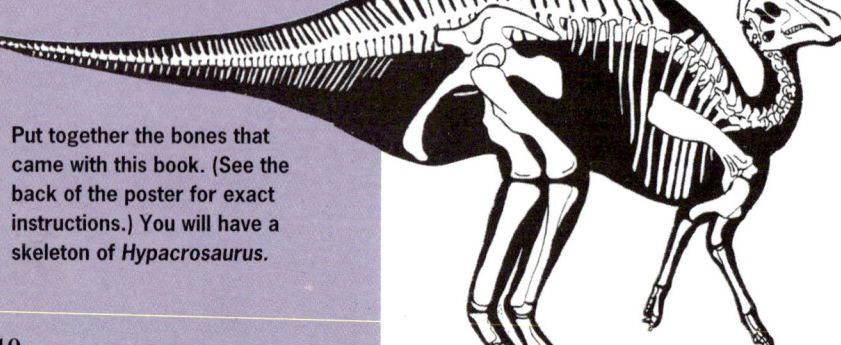

Put together the bones that came with this book. (See the back of the poster for exact instructions.) You will have a skeleton of *Hypacrosaurus*.

Dinosaur "mummies" have also been found. They were formed when a dinosaur's body dried out before it was buried. The skin left a print on the sediments, and the sediments turned to stone. We know, therefore, that *Hypacrosaurus*'s skin was like a pebbly beach, with some bumps larger than others. We also know what food they ate, since the remains of their last meals are sometimes found in the stomach region.

dinosaur skin imprint

closeup

Hypacrosaurus's World

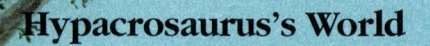

Hypacrosaurus lived at the end of the Mesozoic during a period called the Late Cretaceous. By this time the continents—the big islands of land—were in much the same position as they are today. In the middle of North America was a large, warm, shallow sea surrounded by deltas and swamps. On higher ground were forests of ferns, palms, and pine trees. Flowering plants were becoming numerous, as were birds and mammals.

Hypacrosaurus likely lived in the forest, hidden by the foliage. It ate mostly low plants, up to about six feet (2 m) above ground—about as high as a grown man. To eat especially

tasty bits higher up, it may have stood on its hind legs and reached up with its duck-billed snout.

Joining *Hypacrosaurus* in its foraging were other duck-billed dinosaurs like *Edmontosaurus* (ed-MON-toe-sore-us) and horned dinosaurs like *Anchiceratops* (an-key-i-SERE-ah-tops). Lurking in the shadows were medium-sized tyrannosaurs with their sharp teeth.

Edmontosaurus

Hypacrosaurus

Dinosaur Ducks?

Because *Hypacrosaurus* had a snout like a duck and because the feet of the mummified dinosaurs had what looked like webs, scientists thought that *Hypacrosaurus* paddled about in swamps and lakes. Perhaps the crest on its head was a snorkel or a place to store air when it dived underwater.

These theories made a lot of sense until scientists looked more closely. *Hypacrosaurus*'s mouth was duck-billed, but its teeth were better suited to tough land plants. Indeed, the food found in the mummified dinosaurs' stomachs was land plants, not the softer water plants. What's more, *Hypacrosaurus*'s crest would have made a poor snorkel because it had

14

no opening at the top. And it would have been a rather puny storage tank. Even the webs on the feet turned out not to be webs but dried-out foot pads.

Hypacrosaurus may have splashed into the water to escape a predator or to cool off on a hot day, but it almost certainly lived on land and ate plants that grew there.

Why a Crest?

If the crest wasn't a snorkel, what was it? There are lots of theories:
- **A signal.** Perhaps the crest was a way for members of one species to recognize each other. After all, there were lots of different duck-billed dinosaurs. Without some sort of sign, they were hard to tell apart.
- **A display.** The crests might have been like a peacock's feathers or a deer's antlers—a way to impress other dinosaurs.

- **A way to tell the girls from the boys.** Perhaps the crests of male hypacrosaurs looked different from those of the females.
- **A big nose.** A good sense of smell would have helped warn munching dinosaurs of the approach of another dinosaur that hoped to munch on them.
- **A trumpet.** One of the most interesting theories is that the crest was like a built-in musical instrument. *Hypacrosaurus* could blow through the hollow spaces and make noise.

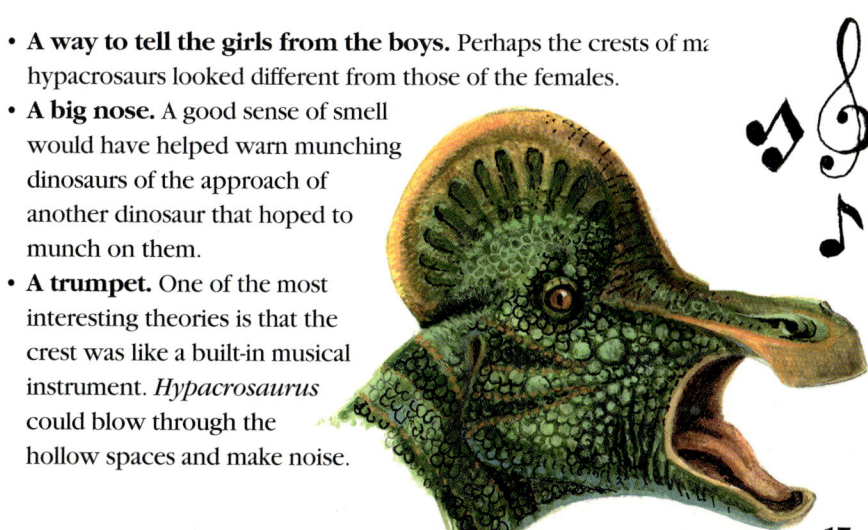

Honk, Honk

To test the idea that hadrosaurs' hollow crests helped them to make noise, David Weishampel, a professor at Johns Hopkins University, built a copy of the crest. Sure enough, when he blew in one end, a noise came out the other.

The tubes in their crests help hadrosaurs make noise the same way that a trumpet or a bassoon works. The mouthpiece of these instruments makes only a small squawk. But as the vibrations travel through the tubes they get louder and lower in tone.

Hypacrosaurus likely made a low honking noise. This noise might have helped it to communicate with its young or to warn other hypacrosaurs of danger.

Most scientists think that the crest was primarily a way these dinosaurs could tell one species from another since all hadrosaurs had crests, but each kind had a unique shape. However, the other possibilities are also likely.

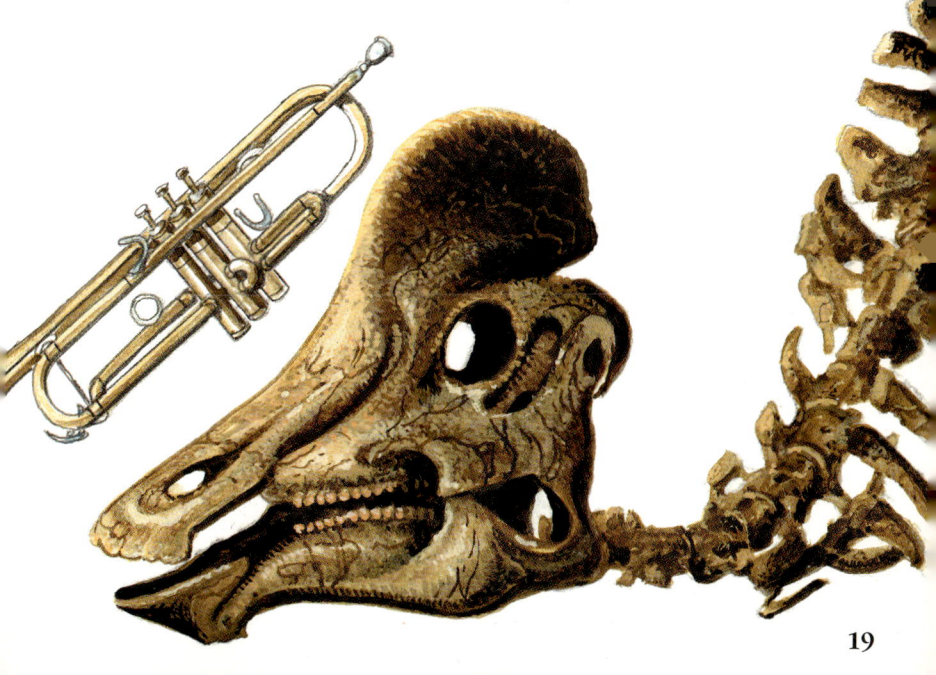

Survival of the Fittest

During the millions of years that living creatures have inhabited the earth, many different kinds have come and gone. Some stayed for only a short time. Others, like frogs and cockroaches, were here before the dinosaurs and are still around today.

These different plants and animals don't just appear out of nowhere. They evolve slowly from earlier forms. In the nineteenth century a man named Charles Darwin developed a theory called natural selection that explains why some living things survive and others don't. He said that the "fittest" survive. We may think that the fittest are the strongest, fastest, or smartest, and this is often true.

However, some are better protected by plates or spines, or can survive longer without food. The fittest are those that are best suited to their surroundings. Mammals, our ancestors, survived during the Age of Dinosaurs because they were small, mouselike creatures that came out only at night.

Hypacrosaurus survived very well for four million years. Why? It was fast, but not the fastest. It was big, but not the biggest. What do you think made *Hypacrosaurus* one of the "fittest"?

All the Better to Eat With

Hypacrosaurus was a big animal and needed a lot of food. And since the food it ate wasn't very nutritious, it had to eat up to sixty pounds (30 kg) of food a day. To help them eat, these dinosaurs had an amazing number of teeth—hundreds and hundreds. When you lose your twenty-eight baby teeth, you grow another set of thirty-two. Instead of thirty-two, *Hypacrosaurus* had one hundred and sixty teeth. And as these teeth wore out, they were continually replaced. All together, the teeth formed a rough surface like a cheese grater.

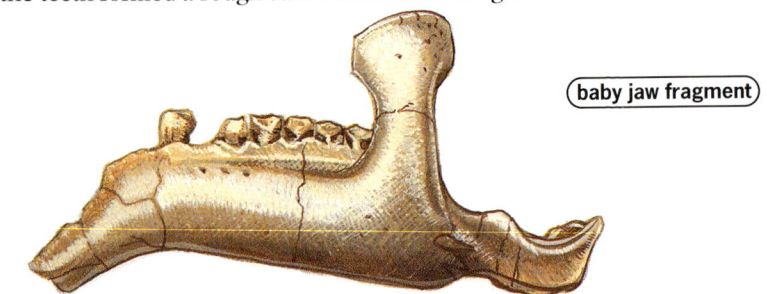

baby jaw fragment

In the front of its long snout, *Hypacrosaurus* had no teeth, just a beak to break off plants. All the teeth were in rows along the sides of its jaw.

To chew, *Hypacrosaurus* didn't move its jaws side to side, as we do, or front to back, as other animals do. Instead, the top teeth slid down the outside of the lower teeth as scissors do when they cut through paper. As the two filelike surfaces rubbed together, they could shred even the toughest plants.

To help further digest its food, *Hypacrosaurus* had a large stomach. Chewed-up food stayed there and fermented.

There may have been so many hypacrosaurs because they were such good eaters and their food was plentiful.

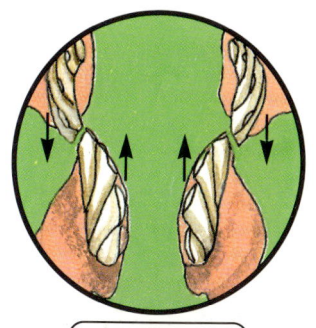

scissorlike teeth

Getting Around

Hypacrosaurus's skeleton tells us a lot about how it moved. Its long, thick hind legs with strong ankles were like pillars that could support all of its weight. The three spade-shaped toes were splayed (spread apart) for a good grip and for better balance. The front legs were shorter, but three of the four fingers were wrapped in a "mitten," making them good for walking on but not for picking up plants or for defense.

To help it walk on two legs, *Hypacrosaurus* had a long, thick tail for balance. The tendons connected to the tall ridge on its spine also helped it keep its body from sagging in the front and back. The ridge strengthened its spine in much the same way that the structure of a bridge keeps it from collapsing.

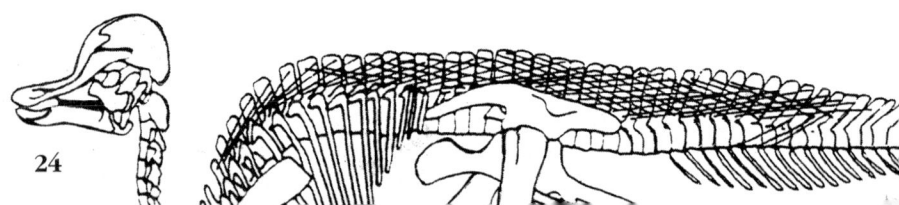

All these clues tell scientists that *Hypacrosaurus* walked on its hind legs and on all fours. When it was in a hurry, it could speed along on two feet at up to twelve miles per hour (20 km/hr). When it was in less of a hurry or just resting or eating low branches, it moved and stood on all fours.

Did *Hypacrosaurus* swim? It could have, but all the signs tell us that it spent most of its time on dry land.

Bringing Up Baby

Like other dinosaurs, *Hypacrosaurus* laid eggs from which its young hatched. Some animals, such as fish or turtles, lay eggs and leave their youngsters to fend for themselves. Other animals, like birds, care for their eggs and for the babies after they hatch.

Hypacrosaurus likely made a nest by squatting in soft earth or sand and turning to carve out a shallow depression. Other females made similar nests nearby. After laying about twenty eggs, *Hypacrosaurus* stayed to protect them from being crushed or eaten by other animals. Since it weighed about 2.2 tons (2 t), *Hypacrosaurus* probably didn't sit on the eggs.

When the babies hatched, they were tiny compared to their parents and weighed only about as much as a human baby. Small and defenseless, they needed their parents to bring food, which was probably carried in the parents' stomachs and then spit into the infants' mouths. The babies grew quickly, however, and at about one month were ready to manage on their own.

When they were old enough, groups of young dinosaurs probably banded together and headed off on their own, coming together perhaps once a year, when they were grown up, to mate and lay their eggs.

Safety in Numbers

Like antelopes or zebras on the plains of Africa today, hypacrosaurs may have lived in large groups or herds. Sometimes, perhaps at breeding time, hypacrosaurs would travel from the forests to other areas, like the sandy shores of lakes. Moving about together gave them protection from predators. They could spot danger with their keen eyesight and hearing, and they could warn each other with their noise-making ability. Thus, at the first hint of danger, the herd could take off in a group, dashing on their strong hind legs, their three-toed feet gripping the ground for speed. As they thundered past, even the hungriest tyrannosaur might think twice about attacking.

And even if one or two weak members of the group were caught or fell, the vast numbers of hypacrosaurs made it to safety, ensuring the survival of the herd.

A Sudden End

Herds of hypacrosaurs once ruled their world. Their amazing survival came about through a combination of efficient eating, speed, and large numbers—and perhaps the ability to "talk" to each other. Then, sixty-five million years ago, something happened to change all that and to bring an end to the Age of Dinosaurs.

No one knows how the last of the dinosaurs died, but many scientists think a comet that struck the earth caused enormous changes around the world. The impact created thick dust that blocked out the sun. Plants died, and without plants, the plant-eating dinosaurs starved to death. The meat-eaters followed soon after. Vaporized rock interacted with the air, producing acid rains and further harming plants and animals.

After that, the world was no longer suited to the dinosaurs. Other plants and animals were now the "fittest," among them mammals, birds, and flowering plants.

Farewell to Hypacrosaurus

We know more about *Hypacrosaurus* than most other dinosaurs. But there is always more to learn about these large, duck-billed creatures, once so well suited to their world.

31